Henry James OM (15 April 1843 – 28 February 1916) was an American-British author regarded as a key transitional figure between literary realism and literary modernism, and is considered by many to be among the greatest novelists in the English language. He was the son of Henry James Sr. and the brother of renowned philosopher and psychologist William James and diarist Alice James.

He is best known for a number of novels dealing with the social and marital interplay between émigré Americans, English people, and continental Europeans. Examples of such novels include The Portrait of a Lady, The Ambassadors, and The Wings of the Dove. His later works were increasingly experimental. In describing the internal states of mind and social dynamics of his characters, James often made use of a style in which ambiguous or contradictory motives and impressions were overlaid or juxtaposed in the discussion of a character's psyche.(Source: Wikipedia)

Literary works:
Watch and Ward (1871)
Roderick Hudson (1875)
The American (1877)
The Europeans (1878)
Confidence (1879)
Washington Square (1880)
The Portrait of a Lady (1881)
The Bostonians (1886)
The Princess Casamassima (1886)
The Reverberator (1888)
The Tragic Muse (1890)
The Other House (1896)
The Spoils of Poynton (1897)
What Maisie Knew (1897)

LOUISA PALLANT

HENRY JAMES

PRINCE CLASSICS

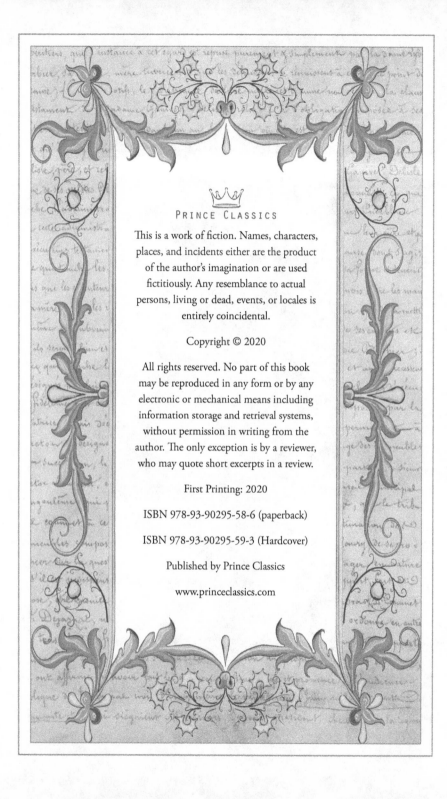

PRINCE CLASSICS

Copyright © 2020

First Printing: 2020

ISBN 978-93-90295-58-6 (paperback)

ISBN 978-93-90295-59-3 (Hardcover)

Published by Prince Classics

www.princeclassics.com

Contents

LOUISA
PALLANT

I

Never say you know the last words about any human heart! I was once treated to a revelation which startled and touched me in the nature of a person with whom I had been acquainted—well, as I supposed—for years, whose character I had had good reasons, heaven knows, to appreciate and in regard to whom I flattered myself I had nothing more to learn.

It was on the terrace of the Kursaal at Homburg, nearly ten years ago, one beautiful night toward the end of July. I had come to the place that day from Frankfort, with vague intentions, and was mainly occupied in waiting for my young nephew, the only son of my sister, who had been entrusted to my care by a very fond mother for the summer—I was expected to show him Europe, only the very best of it—and was on his way from Paris to join me. The excellent band discoursed music not too abstruse, while the air was filled besides with the murmur of different languages, the smoke of many cigars, the creak on the gravel of the gardens of strolling shoes and the thick tinkle of beer-glasses. There were a hundred people walking about, there were some in clusters at little tables and many on benches and rows of chairs, watching the others as if they had paid for the privilege and were rather disappointed. I was among these last; I sat by myself, smoking my cigar and thinking of nothing very particular while families and couples passed and repassed me.

I scarce know how long I had sat when I became aware of a recognition which made my meditations definite. It was on my own part, and the object of it was a lady who moved to and fro, unconscious of my observation, with a young girl at her side. I hadn't seen her for ten years, and what first struck me was the fact not that she was Mrs. Henry Pallant, but that the girl who was with her was remarkably pretty—or rather first of all that every one who passed appeared extremely to admire. This led me also to notice the young lady myself, and her charming face diverted my attention for some time from that of her companion. The latter, moreover, though it was night, wore a thin light veil which made her features vague. The couple slowly walked and walked, but though they were very quiet and decorous, and also very well dressed, they seemed to have no friends. Every one observed but no one addressed them; they appeared even themselves to exchange very few words. Moreover they bore with marked composure and as if they were thoroughly used to it the attention they excited. I am afraid it occurred to me to take for granted that they were of an artful intention and that if they hadn't been the elder lady would have handed the younger over a little less to public valuation and not have sought so to conceal her own face. Perhaps this question came into my mind too easily just then—in view of my prospective mentorship to my nephew. If I was to show him only the best of Europe I should have to be very careful about the people he should meet—especially the ladies—and the relations he should form. I suspected him of great innocence and was uneasy about my office. Was I completely relieved and reassured when I became aware that I simply had Louisa Pallant before me and that the girl was her daughter Linda, whom I had known as a child—Linda grown up to charming beauty?

The question was delicate and the proof that I was not very sure is perhaps that I forbore to speak to my pair at once. I watched them a while—I wondered what they would do. No great harm assuredly; but I was anxious to see if they were really isolated. Homburg was then a great resort of the English—the London season took up its tale there toward the first of August—and I had an idea that in such a company as that Louisa would naturally know people. It was my impression that she "cultivated" the English, that she had been much in London and would be likely to have views in regard to a permanent settlement there. This supposition was quickened by the sight of Linda's beauty, for I knew there is no country in which such attractions are more appreciated. You will see what time I took, and I confess that as I finished my cigar I thought it all over. There was no good reason in fact why I should have rushed into Mrs. Pallant's arms. She had not treated me well and we had never really made it up. Somehow even the circumstance that—after the first soreness—I was glad to have lost her had never put us quite right with each other; nor, for herself, had it made her less ashamed of her heartless behaviour that poor Pallant proved finally no great catch. I had forgiven her; I hadn't felt it anything but an escape not to have married a girl who had in her to take back her given word and break a fellow's heart for mere flesh-pots—or the shallow promise, as it pitifully turned out, of flesh-pots. Moreover we had met since then—on the occasion of my former visit to Europe; had looked each other in the eyes, had pretended to be easy friends and had talked of the wickedness of the world as composedly as if we were the only just, the only pure. I knew by that time what she had given out—that I had driven her off by my insane jealousy before she ever thought of Henry Pallant, before she had ever seen him. This hadn't been before and couldn't be to-day a ground of real reunion, especially if you add to it that she knew perfectly what I thought of her. It seldom ministers to friendship, I believe, that your friend shall know your real opinion, for he knows it mainly when it's unfavourable, and this is especially the case if—let the solecism pass!—he be a woman. I hadn't followed Mrs. Pallant's fortunes; the years went by for me in my own country, whereas she led her life, which I vaguely believed to be difficult after her husband's death—virtually that of a bankrupt—in foreign lands. I heard of her from time to time; always as "established" somewhere, but on each occasion in a different place. She drifted from country to country, and if she had been of a hard composition at the beginning it could never occur to me that her struggle with society, as it might be called, would have softened the paste. Whenever I heard a woman spoken of as "horribly worldly" I thought immediately of the object of my early passion. I imagined she had debts, and when I now at last made up my mind to recall myself to her it was present to me that she might ask me to lend her money. More than anything else, however, at this time of day, I was sorry for her, so that such an idea didn't operate as a deterrent.

She pretended afterwards that she hadn't noticed me—expressing as we stood face to face great surprise and wishing to know where I had dropped from; but I think the corner of her eye had taken me in and she had been waiting to see what I would do. She had ended by sitting down with her girl on the same row of chairs with myself, and after a little, the seat next to her becoming vacant, I had gone and stood before her. She had then looked up at me a moment, staring as if she couldn't imagine who I was or what I wanted; after which, smiling and extending her hands, she had broken out: "Ah my dear old friend—what a delight!" If she had waited to see what I would do in order to choose her own line she thus at least carried out this line with the utmost grace. She was cordial, friendly, artless, interested, and indeed I'm sure she was very glad to see me. I may as well say immediately, none the less, that she gave me neither then nor later any sign of a desire to contract a loan. She had scant means—that I learned—yet seemed for the moment able to pay her way. I took the empty chair and we remained in talk for an hour. After a while she made me sit at her other side, next her daughter, whom she wished to know me—to love me—as one of their oldest friends. "It goes back, back, back, doesn't it?" said Mrs. Pallant; "and of course she remembers you as a child." Linda smiled all sweetly and blankly, and I saw she remembered me not a whit. When her mother threw out that they had often talked about me she failed to take it up, though she looked extremely nice. Looking nice was her strong point; she was prettier even than her mother had been. She was such a little lady that she made me ashamed of having doubted, however vaguely and for a moment, of her position in the scale of propriety. Her appearance seemed to say that if she had no acquaintances it was because she didn't want them—because nobody there struck her as attractive: there wasn't the slightest difficulty about her choosing her friends. Linda Pallant, young as she was, and fresh and fair and charming, gentle and sufficiently shy, looked somehow exclusive—as if the dust of the common world had never been meant to besprinkle her. She was of thinner consistency than her mother and clearly not a young woman of professions—except in so far as she was committed to an interest in you by her bright pure candid smile. No girl who had such a lovely way of parting her lips could pass for designing.

As I sat between the pair I felt I had been taken possession of and that for better or worse my stay at Homburg would be intimately associated with theirs. We gave each other a great deal of news and expressed unlimited interest in each other's history since our last meeting. I mightn't judge of what Mrs. Pallant kept back, but for myself I quite overflowed. She let me see at any rate that her life had been a good deal what I supposed, though the terms she employed to describe it were less crude than those of my thought. She confessed they had drifted, she and her daughter, and were drifting still. Her narrative rambled and took a wrong turn, a false flight, or two, as I thought Linda noted, while she sat watching the passers, in a manner that betrayed no consciousness of their attention, without coming to her mother's aid. Once or twice Mrs. Pallant made me rather feel a cross-questioner, which I had had no intention of being. I took it that if the girl never put in a word it was because she had perfect confidence in her parent's ability to come out straight. It was suggested to me, I scarcely knew how, that this confidence between the two ladies went to a great length; that their union of thought, their system of reciprocal divination, was remarkable, and that they probably seldom needed to resort to the clumsy and in some cases dangerous expedient of communicating by sound. I suppose I made this reflexion not all at once— it was not wholly the result of that first meeting. I was with them constantly for the next several days and my impressions had time to clarify.

I do remember, however, that it was on this first evening that Archie's name came up. She attributed her own stay at Homburg to no refined nor exalted motive—didn't put it that she was there from force of habit or because a high medical authority had ordered her to drink the waters; she frankly admitted the reason of her visit to have been simply that she didn't know where else to turn. But she appeared to assume that my behaviour rested on higher grounds and even that it required explanation, the place being frivolous and modern—devoid of that interest of antiquity which I had ever made so much of. "Don't you remember—ever so long ago—that you wouldn't look at anything in Europe that wasn't a thousand years old? Well, as we advance in life I suppose we don't think that quite such a charm." And when I mentioned that I had arrived because the place was as good as another for awaiting my nephew she exclaimed: "Your nephew—what nephew? He must have come up of late." I answered that his name was Archie Parker and that he was modern indeed; he was to attain legal manhood in a few months and was in Europe for the first time. My last news of him had been from Paris and I was expecting to hear further from one day to the other. His father was dead, and though a selfish bachelor, little versed in the care of children, I was considerably counted on by his mother to see that he didn't smoke nor flirt too much, nor yet tumble off an Alp.

Mrs. Pallant immediately guessed that his mother was my sister Charlotte, whom she spoke of familiarly, though I knew she had scarce seen her. Then in a moment it came to her which of the Parkers Charlotte had married; she remembered the family perfectly from the old New York days—"that disgustingly rich set." She said it was very nice having the boy come out that way to my care; to which I replied that it was very nice for the boy. She pronounced the advantage rather mine—I ought to have had children; there was something so parental about me and I would have brought them up so well. She could make an allusion like that—to all that might have been and had not been—without a gleam of guilt in her eye; and I foresaw that before I left the place I should have confided to her that though I detested her and was very glad we had fallen out, yet our old relations had left me no heart for marrying another woman. If I had remained so single and so sterile the fault was nobody's but hers. She asked what I meant to do with my nephew—to which I replied that it was much more a question of what he would do with me. She wished to know if he were a nice young man and had brothers and sisters and any particular profession. I assured her I had really seen little of him; I believed him to be six feet high and of tolerable parts. He was an only son, but there was a little sister at home, a delicate, rather blighted child, demanding all the mother's care.

"So that makes your responsibility greater, as it were, about the boy, doesn't it?" said Mrs. Pallant.

"Greater? I'm sure I don't know."

"Why if the girl's life's uncertain he may become, some moment, all the mother has. So that being in your hands—"

"Oh I shall keep him alive, I suppose, if you mean that," I returned.

"Well, WE won't kill him, shall we, Linda?" my friend went on with a laugh.

"I don't know—perhaps we shall!" smiled the girl.

II

I called on them the next at their lodgings, the modesty of which was enhanced by a hundred pretty feminine devices—flowers and photographs and portable knick-knacks and a hired piano and morsels of old brocade flung over angular sofas. I took them to drive; I met them again at the Kursaal; I arranged that we should dine together, after the Homburg fashion, at the same table d'hote; and during several days this revived familiar intercourse continued, imitating intimacy if not quite achieving it. I was pleased, as my companions passed the time for me and the conditions of our life were soothing—the feeling of summer and shade and music and leisure in the German gardens and woods, where we strolled and sat and gossiped; to which may be added a vague sociable sense that among people whose challenge to the curiosity was mainly not irresistible we kept quite to ourselves. We were on the footing of old friends who still had in regard to each other discoveries to make. We knew each other's nature but didn't know each other's experience; so that when Mrs. Pallant related to me what she had been "up to," as I called it, for so many years, the former knowledge attached a hundred interpretative footnotes—as if I had been editing an author who presented difficulties—to the interesting page. There was nothing new to me in the fact that I didn't esteem her, but there was relief in my finding that this wasn't necessary at Homburg and that I could like her in spite of it. She struck me, in the oddest way, as both improved and degenerate; the two processes, in her nature, might have gone on together. She was battered and world-worn and, spiritually speaking, vulgarised; something fresh had rubbed off her—it even included the vivacity of her early desire to do the best thing for herself— and something rather stale had rubbed on. At the same time she betrayed a scepticism, and that was rather becoming, for it had quenched the eagerness of her prime, the mercenary principle I had so suffered from. She had grown weary and detached, and since she affected me as more impressed with the evil of the world than with the good, this was a gain; in other words her accretion of indifference, if not of cynicism, showed a softer surface than that of her old ambitions. Furthermore I had to recognise that her devotion to her daughter was a kind of religion; she had done the very best possible for Linda.

Linda was curious, Linda was interesting; I've seen girls I liked better—charming as this one might be—but have never seen one who for the hour you were with her (the impression passed somehow when she was out of sight) occupied you so completely. I can best describe the attention she provoked by saying that she struck you above all things as a felicitous FINAL product—after the fashion of some plant or some fruit, some waxen orchid or some perfect peach. She was clearly the result of a process of calculation, a process patiently educative, a pressure exerted, and all artfully, so that she should reach a high point.

This high point had been the star of her mother's heaven—it hung before her so unquenchably—and had shed the only light (in default of a better) that was to shine on the poor lady's path. It stood her instead of every other ideal. The very most and the very best—that was what the girl had been led on to achieve; I mean of course, since no real miracle had been wrought, the most and the best she was capable of. She was as pretty, as graceful, as intelligent, as well-bred, as well-informed, as well-dressed, as could have been conceived for her; her music, her singing, her German, her French, her English, her step, her tone, her glance, her manner, everything in her person and movement, from the shade and twist of her hair to the way you saw her finger-nails were pink when she raised her hand, had been carried so far that one found one's self accepting them as the very measure of young grace. I regarded her thus as a model, yet it was a part of her perfection that she had none of the stiffness of a pattern. If she held the observation it was because you wondered where and when she would break down; but she never broke down, either in her French accent or in her role of educated angel.

After Archie had come the ladies were manifestly his greatest resource, and all the world knows why a party of four is more convenient than a party of three. My nephew had kept me waiting a week, with a serenity all his own; but this very coolness was a help to harmony—so long, that is, as I didn't lose my temper with it. I didn't, for the most part, because my young man's unperturbed acceptance of the most various forms of good fortune had more than anything else the effect of amusing me. I had seen little of him for the last three or four years; I wondered what his impending majority would have made of him—he didn't at all carry himself as if the wind of his fortune were rising—and I watched him with a solicitude that usually ended in a joke. He was a tall fresh-coloured youth, with a candid circular countenance and a love of cigarettes, horses and boats which had not been sacrificed to more strenuous studies. He was reassuringly natural, in a supercivilised age, and I soon made up my mind that the formula of his character was in the clearing of the inward scene by his so preordained lack of imagination. If he was serene this was still further simplifying. After that I had time to meditate on the line that divides the serene from the inane, the simple from the silly. He wasn't clever; the fonder theory quite defied our cultivation, though Mrs. Pallant tried it once or twice; but on the other hand it struck me his want of wit might be a good defensive weapon. It wasn't the sort of density that would let him in, but the sort that would keep him out. By which I don't mean that he had shortsighted suspicions, but that on the contrary imagination would never be needed to save him, since she would never put him in danger. He was in short a well-grown well-washed muscular young American, whose extreme salubrity might have made him pass for conceited. If he looked pleased with himself it was only because he was pleased with life—as well he might be, with the fortune that awaited the stroke of his twenty-first year—and his big healthy independent person was an inevitable part of that. I am bound to add that he was accommodating—for which I was grateful. His habits were active, but he didn't insist on my adopting them and he made numerous and generous sacrifices for my society. When I say he made them for mine I must duly remember that mine and that of Mrs. Pallant and Linda were now very much the same thing. He was willing to sit and smoke for hours under the trees or, adapting his long legs to the pace of his three companions, stroll through the nearer woods of the charming little hill-range of the Taunus to those rustic Wirthschaften where coffee might be drunk under a trellis. Mrs. Pallant took a great interest in him; she made him, with his easy uncle, a subject of discourse; she pronounced him a delightful specimen, as a young gentleman of his period and country. She even asked me the sort of "figure" his fortune might really amount to, and professed a rage of envy when I

17

told her what I supposed it to be. While we were so occupied Archie, on his side, couldn't do less than converse with Linda, nor to tell the truth did he betray the least inclination for any different exercise. They strolled away together while their elders rested; two or three times, in the evening, when the ballroom of the Kursaal was lighted and dance-music played, they whirled over the smooth floor in a waltz that stirred my memory. Whether it had the same effect on Mrs. Pallant's I know not: she held her peace. We had on certain occasions our moments, almost our half-hours, of unembarrassed silence while our young companions disported themselves. But if at other times her enquiries and comments were numerous on this article of my ingenuous charge, that might very well have passed for a courteous recognition of the frequent admiration I expressed for Linda—an admiration that drew from her, I noticed, but scant direct response. I was struck thus with her reserve when I spoke of her daughter—my remarks produced so little of a maternal flutter. Her detachment, her air of having no fatuous illusions and not being blinded by prejudice, seemed to me at times to savour of affectation. Either she answered me with a vague and impatient sigh and changed the subject, or else she said before doing so: "Oh yes, yes, she's a very brilliant creature. She ought to be: God knows what I've done for her!" The reader will have noted my fondness, in all cases, for the explanations of things; as an example of which I had my theory here that she was disappointed in the girl. Where then had her special calculation failed? As she couldn't possibly have wished her prettier or more pleasing, the pang must have been for her not having made a successful use of her gifts. Had she expected her to "land" a prince the day after leaving the schoolroom? There was after all plenty of time for this, with Linda but two-and-twenty. It didn't occur to me to wonder if the source of her mother's tepidity was that the young lady had not turned out so nice a nature as she had hoped, because in the first place Linda struck me as perfectly innocent, and because in the second I wasn't paid, in the French phrase, for supposing Louisa Pallant much concerned on that score. The last hypothesis I should have invoked was that of private despair at bad moral symptoms. And in relation to Linda's nature I had before me the daily spectacle of her manner with my nephew. It was as charming as it could be without betrayal of a desire to lead him on. She was as familiar as a cousin, but as a distant one—a cousin who had been brought up to observe degrees. She was so much cleverer than Archie that she couldn't help laughing at him, but she didn't laugh enough to exclude variety, being well aware, no doubt, that a woman's cleverness most shines in contrast with a man's stupidity when she pretends to take that stupidity for her law. Linda Pallant moreover was not a chatterbox; as she knew the value of many things she knew the value of intervals. There were a good many in the conversation of these young persons; my nephew's own speech, to say nothing of his thought, abounding in comfortable lapses; so that I sometimes wondered how their association was kept at that pitch of continuity of which it gave the impression. It was friendly enough, evidently, when Archie sat near her—near enough for low murmurs, had such risen to his lips—and watched her with interested eyes and with freedom not to try too hard to make himself agreeable. She had always something in hand—a flower in her tapestry to finish, the leaves of a magazine to cut, a button to sew on her glove (she carried a little work-bag in her pocket and was a person of the daintiest habits), a pencil to ply ever so neatly in a sketchbook which she rested on her knee. When we were indoors—mainly then at her mother's modest rooms—she had always the resource of her piano, of which she was of course a perfect mistress.

These pursuits supported her, they helped her to an assurance under such narrow inspection—I ended by rebuking Archie for it; I told him he stared the poor girl out of countenance—and she sought further relief in smiling all over the place. When my young man's eyes shone at her those of Miss Pallant addressed themselves brightly to the trees and clouds and other surrounding objects, including her mother and me. Sometimes she broke into a sudden embarrassed happy pointless laugh. When she wandered off with him she looked back at us in a manner that promised it wasn't for long and that she was with us still in spirit. If I liked her I had therefore my good reason: it was many a day since a pretty girl had had the air of taking me so much into account. Sometimes when they were so far away as not to disturb us she read aloud a little to Mr. Archie. I don't know where she got her books—I never provided them, and certainly he didn't. He was no reader and I fear he often dozed.

III

I remember the first time—it was at the end of about ten days of this—that Mrs. Pallant remarked to me: "My dear friend, you're quite AMAZING! You behave for all the world as if you were perfectly ready to accept certain consequences." She nodded in the direction of our young companions, but I nevertheless put her at the pains of saying what consequences she meant. "What consequences? Why the very same consequences that ensued when you and I first became acquainted."

I hesitated, but then, looking her in the eyes, said: "Do you mean she'd throw him over?"

"You're not kind, you're not generous," she replied with a quick colour. "I'm giving you a warning."

"You mean that my boy may fall in love with your girl?"

"Certainly. It looks even as if the harm might be already done."

"Then your warning comes too late," I significantly smiled. "But why do you call it a harm?"

"Haven't you any sense of the rigour of your office?" she asked. "Is that what his mother has sent him out to you for: that you shall find him the first wife you can pick up, that you shall let him put his head into the noose the day after his arrival?"

"Heaven forbid I should do anything of the kind! I know moreover that his mother doesn't want him to marry young. She holds it the worst of mistakes, she feels that at that age a man never really chooses. He doesn't choose till he has lived a while, till he has looked about and compared."

"And what do you think then yourself?"

"I should like to say I regard the fact of falling in love, at whatever age, as in itself an act of selection. But my being as I am at this time of day would contradict me too much."

"Well then, you're too primitive. You ought to leave this place tomorrow."

"So as not to see Archie fall—?"

"You ought to fish him out now—from where he HAS fallen—and take him straight away."

I wondered a little. "Do you think he's in very far?"

"If I were his mother I know what I should think. I can put myself in her place—I'm not narrow-minded. I know perfectly well how she must regard such a question."

"And don't you know," I returned, "that in America that's not thought important—the way the mother regards it?"

Mrs. Pallant had a pause—as if I mystified or vexed her. "Well, we're not in America. We happen to be here."

"No; my poor sister's up to her neck in New York."

"I'm almost capable of writing to her to come out," said Mrs. Pallant.

"You ARE warning me," I cried, "but I hardly know of what! It seems to me my responsibility would begin only at the moment your daughter herself should seem in danger."

"Oh you needn't mind that—I'll take care of Linda."

But I went on. "If you think she's in danger already I'll carry him off to-morrow."

"It would be the best thing you could do."

"I don't know—I should be very sorry to act on a false alarm. I'm very well here; I like the place and the life and your society. Besides, it doesn't strike me that—on her side—there's any real symptom."

She looked at me with an air I had never seen in her face, and if I had puzzled her she repaid me in kind. "You're very annoying. You don't deserve what I'd fain do for you."

21

What she'd fain do for me she didn't tell me that day, but we took up the subject again. I remarked that I failed to see why we should assume that a girl like Linda—brilliant enough to make one of the greatest—would fall so very easily into my nephew's arms. Might I enquire if her mother had won a confession from her, if she had stammered out her secret? Mrs. Pallant made me, on this, the point that they had no need to tell each other such things—they hadn't lived together twenty years in such intimacy for nothing. To which I returned that I had guessed as much, but that there might be an exception for a great occasion like the present. If Linda had shown nothing it was a sign that for HER the occasion wasn't great; and I mentioned that Archie had spoken to me of the young lady only to remark casually and rather patronisingly, after his first encounter with her, that she was a regular little flower. (The little flower was nearly three years older than himself.) Apart from this he hadn't alluded to her and had taken up no allusion of mine. Mrs. Pallant informed me again—for which I was prepared—that I was quite too primitive; after which she said: "We needn't discuss the case if you don't wish to, but I happen to know—how I obtained my knowledge isn't important— that the moment Mr. Parker should propose to my daughter she'd gobble him down. Surely it's a detail worth mentioning to you."

I sought to defer then to her judgement. "Very good. I'll sound him. I'll look into the matter tonight."

"Don't, don't; you'll spoil everything!" She spoke as with some finer view. "Remove him quickly—that's the only thing."

I didn't at all like the idea of removing him quickly; it seemed too summary, too extravagant, even if presented to him on specious grounds; and moreover, as I had told Mrs. Pallant, I really had no wish to change my scene. It was no part of my promise to my sister that, with my middle-aged habits, I should duck and dodge about Europe. So I temporised. "Should you really object to the boy so much as a son-in-law? After all he's a good fellow and a gentleman."

"My poor friend, you're incredibly superficial!" she made answer with an assurance that struck me.

The contempt in it so nettled me in fact that I exclaimed: "Possibly! But it seems odd that a lesson in consistency should come from YOU."

I had no retort from her on this, rather to my surprise, and when she spoke again it was all quietly. "I think Linda and I had best withdraw. We've been here a month—it will have served our purpose."

"Mercy on us, that will be a bore!" I protested; and for the rest of the evening, till we separated—our conversation had taken place after dinner at the Kursaal—she said little, preserving a subdued and almost injured air. This somehow didn't appeal to me, since it was absurd that Louisa Pallant, of all women, should propose to put me in the wrong. If ever a woman had been in the wrong herself—! I had even no need to go into that. Archie and I, at all events, usually attended the ladies back to their own door—they lived in a street of minor accommodation at a certain distance from the Rooms— where we parted for the night late, on the big cobblestones, in the little sleeping German town, under the closed windows of which, suggesting stuffy interiors, our cheerful English partings resounded. On this occasion indeed they rather languished; the question that had come up for me with Mrs. Pallant appeared—and by no intention of mine—to have brushed the young couple with its chill. Archie and Linda too struck me as conscious and dumb.

As I walked back to our hotel with my nephew I passed my hand into his arm and put to him, by no roundabout approach, the question of whether he were in serious peril of love.

"I don't know, I don't know—really, uncle, I don't know!" was, however, all the satisfaction I could extract from the youth, who hadn't the smallest vein of introspection. He mightn't know, but before we reached the inn—we had a few more words on the subject—it seemed to me that *I* did. His mind wasn't formed to accommodate at one time many subjects of thought, but Linda Pallant certainly constituted for the moment its principal furniture. She pervaded his consciousness, she solicited his curiosity, she associated herself, in a manner as yet informal and undefined, with his future. I could see that she held, that she beguiled him as no one had ever done. I didn't betray to him, however, that perception, and I spent my night a prey to the

23

consciousness that, after all, it had been none of my business to provide him with the sense of being captivated. To put him in relation with a young enchantress was the last thing his mother had expected of me or that I had expected of myself. Moreover it was quite my opinion that he himself was too young to be a judge of enchantresses. Mrs. Pallant was right and I had given high proof of levity in regarding her, with her beautiful daughter, as a "resource." There were other resources—one of which WOULD be most decidedly to clear out. What did I know after all about the girl except that I rejoiced to have escaped from marrying her mother? That mother, it was true, was a singular person, and it was strange her conscience should have begun to fidget in advance of my own. It was strange she should so soon have felt Archie's peril, and even stranger that she should have then wished to "save" him. The ways of women were infinitely subtle, and it was no novelty to me that one never knew where they would turn up. As I haven't hesitated in this report to expose the irritable side of my own nature I shall confess that I even wondered if my old friend's solicitude hadn't been a deeper artifice. Wasn't it possibly a plan of her own for making sure of my young man—though I didn't quite see the logic of it? If she regarded him, which she might in view of his large fortune, as a great catch, mightn't she have arranged this little comedy, in their personal interest, with the girl?

That possibility at any rate only made it a happier thought that I should win my companion to some curiosity about other places. There were many of course much more worth his attention than Homburg. In the course of the morning—it was after our early luncheon—I walked round to Mrs. Pallant's to let her know I was ready to take action; but even while I went I again felt the unlikelihood of the part attributed by my fears and by the mother's own, so far as they had been roused, to Linda. Certainly if she was such a girl as these fears represented her she would fly at higher game. It was with an eye to high game, Mrs. Pallant had frankly admitted to me, that she had been trained, and such an education, to say nothing of such a performer, justified a hope of greater returns. A young American, the fruit of scant "modelling," who could give her nothing but pocket-money, was a very moderate prize, and if she had been prepared to marry for ambition—there was no such hardness in her face or tone, but then there never is—her mark would be inevitably a "personage" quelconque. I was received at my friend's lodging with the announcement that she had left Homburg with her daughter half an hour before. The good woman who had entertained the pair professed to know nothing of their movements beyond the fact that they had gone to Frankfort, where, however, it was her belief that they didn't intend to remain. They were evidently travelling beyond. Sudden, their decision to move? Oh yes, the matter of a moment. They must have spent the night in packing, they had so many things and such pretty ones; and their poor maid, all the morning, had scarce had time to swallow her coffee. But they clearly were ladies accustomed to come and go. It didn't matter—with such rooms as hers she never wanted: there was a new family coming in at three.

IV

This piece of strategy left me staring and made me, I must confess, quite furious. My only consolation was that Archie, when I told him, looked as blank as myself, and that the trick touched him more nearly, for I was not now in love with Louisa. We agreed that we required an explanation and we pretended to expect one the next day in the shape of a letter satisfactory even to the point of being apologetic. When I say "we" pretended I mean that I did, for my suspicion that he knew what had been on foot—through an arrangement with Linda—lasted only a moment. If his resentment was less than my own his surprise was equally great. I had been willing to bolt, but I felt slighted by the ease with which Mrs. Pallant had shown she could part with us. Archie professed no sense of a grievance, because in the first place he was shy about it and because in the second it was evidently not definite to him that he had been encouraged—equipped as he was, I think, with no very particular idea of what constituted encouragement. He was fresh from the wonderful country in which there may between the ingenuous young be so little question of "intentions." He was but dimly conscious of his own and could by no means have told me whether he had been challenged or been jilted. I didn't want to exasperate him, but when at the end of three days more we were still without news of our late companions I observed that it was very simple:—they must have been just hiding from us; they thought us dangerous; they wished to avoid entanglements. They had found us too attentive and wished not to raise false hopes. He appeared to accept this explanation and even had the air—so at least I inferred from his asking me no questions—of judging the matter might be delicate for myself. The poor youth was altogether much mystified, and I smiled at the image in his mind of Mrs. Pallant fleeing from his uncle's importunities. We decided to leave Homburg, but if we didn't pursue our fugitives it wasn't simply that we were ignorant of where they were. I could have found that out with a little trouble, but I was deterred by the reflexion that this would be Louisa's reasoning. She was a dreadful humbug and her departure had been a provocation—I fear it was in that stupid conviction that I made out a little independent itinerary with Archie. I even believed we should learn where they were quite soon enough, and that our patience—even my young man's—would be longer than theirs. Therefore I uttered a small private cry of triumph when three weeks later—we happened to be at Interlaken—he reported to me that he had received a note from Miss Pallant. The form of this confidence was his enquiring if there were particular reasons why we should longer delay our projected visit to the Italian lakes. Mightn't the fear of the hot weather, which was moreover at that season our native temperature, cease to operate, the middle of September having arrived? I answered that we would start on the morrow if he liked, and then, pleased apparently that I was so easy to deal with, he revealed his little secret. He showed me his letter, which was a graceful natural document—it covered with a few flowing strokes but a single page of note-paper—not at all compromising to the young lady. If, however, it was almost the apology I had looked for—save that this should have come from the mother—it was not ostensibly in the least an invitation. It mentioned casually—the mention was mainly in the words at the head of her paper—that they were on the Lago Maggiore, at Baveno; but it consisted mainly of the expression of a regret that they had had so abruptly to leave Homburg. Linda failed to say under what necessity they had found themselves; she only hoped we hadn't judged them too harshly and would accept "this hasty line" as a substitute for the omitted good-bye. She also hoped our days were passing pleasantly and with the same lovely weather that prevailed south of the Alps; and she remained very sincerely and with the kindest remembrances—!

The note contained no message from her mother, and it was open to me to suppose, as I should prefer, either that Mrs. Pallant hadn't known she was writing or that they wished to make us think she hadn't known. The letter might pass as a common civility of the girl's to a person with whom she had been on easy terms. It was, however, for something more than this that my nephew took it; so at least I gathered from the touching candour of his determination to go to Baveno. I judged it idle to drag him another way; he had money in his own pocket and was quite capable of giving me the slip. Yet—such are the sweet incongruities of youth—when I asked him to what tune he had been thinking of Linda since they left us in the lurch he replied:

"Oh I haven't been thinking at all! Why should I?" This fib was accompanied by an exorbitant blush. Since he was to obey his young woman's signal I must equally make out where it would take him, and one splendid morning we started over the Simplon in a post-chaise.

I represented to him successfully that it would be in much better taste for us to alight at Stresa, which as every one knows is a resort of tourists, also on the shore of the major lake, at about a mile's distance from Baveno. If we stayed at the latter place we should have to inhabit the same hotel as our friends, and this might be awkward in view of a strained relation with them. Nothing would be easier than to go and come between the two points, especially by the water, which would give Archie a chance for unlimited paddling. His face lighted up at the vision of a pair of oars; he pretended to take my plea for discretion very seriously, and I could see that he had at once begun to calculate opportunities for navigation with Linda. Our post-chaise—I had insisted on easy stages and we were three days on the way—deposited us at Stresa toward the middle of the afternoon, and it was within an amazingly short time that I found myself in a small boat with my nephew, who pulled us over to Baveno with vigorous strokes. I remember the sweetness of the whole impression. I had had it before, but to my companion it was new, and he thought it as pretty as the opera: the enchanting beauty of the place and, hour, the stillness of the air and water, with the romantic fantastic Borromean Islands set as great jewels in a crystal globe. We disembarked at the steps by the garden-foot of the hotel, and somehow it seemed a perfectly natural part of the lovely situation that I should immediately become conscious of Mrs. Pallant and her daughter seated on the terrace and quietly watching us. They had the air of expectation, which I think we had counted on. I hadn't even asked Archie if he had answered Linda's note; this was between themselves and in the way of supervision I had done enough in coming with him.

There is no doubt our present address, all round, lacked a little the easiest grace—or at least Louisa's and mine did. I felt too much the appeal of her exhibition to notice closely the style of encounter of the young people. I couldn't get it out of my head, as I have sufficiently indicated, that Mrs. Pallant was playing a game, and I'm afraid she saw in my face that this suspicion had been the motive of my journey. I had come there to find her out. The knowledge of my purpose couldn't help her to make me very welcome, and that's why I speak of our meeting constrainedly. We observed none the less all the forms, and the admirable scene left us plenty to talk about. I made no reference before Linda to the retreat from Homburg. This young woman looked even prettier than she had done on the eve of that manoeuvre and gave no sign of an awkward consciousness. She again so struck me as a charming clever girl that I was freshly puzzled to know why we should get—or should have got—into a tangle about her. People had to want to complicate a situation to do it on so simple a pretext as that Linda was in every way beautiful. This was the clear fact: so why shouldn't the presumptions be in favour of every result of it? One of the effects of that cause, on the spot, was that at the end of a very short time Archie proposed to her to take a turn with him in his boat, which awaited us at the foot of the steps. She looked at her mother with a smiling "May I, mamma?" and Mrs. Pallant answered, "Certainly, darling, if you're not afraid." At this—I scarcely knew why—I sought the relief of laughter: it must have affected me as comic that the girl's general competence should suffer the imputation of that particular flaw. She gave me a quick slightly sharp look as she turned away with my nephew; it appeared to challenge me a little—"Pray what's the matter with YOU?" It was the first expression of the kind I had ever seen in her face. Mrs. Pallant's attention, on the other hand, rather strayed from me; after we had been left there together she sat silent, not heeding me, looking at the lake and mountains—at the snowy crests crowned with the flush of evening. She seemed not even to follow our young companions as they got into their boat and pushed off. For some minutes I respected her mood; I walked slowly up and down the terrace and lighted a cigar, as she had always permitted me to do at Homburg. I found in her, it was true, rather a new air of weariness; her fine cold well-bred face was pale; I noted in it new lines of fatigue, almost of age. At last I stopped in front of her and—since she looked so sad—asked if she had been having bad news.

"The only bad news was when I learned—through your nephew's note to Linda—that you were coming to us."

"Ah then he wrote?"

"Certainly he wrote."

"You take it all harder than I do," I returned as I sat down beside her. And then I added, smiling: "Have you written to his mother?"

Slowly at last, and more directly, she faced me. "Take care, take care, or you'll have been more brutal than you'll afterwards like," she said with an air of patience before the inevitable.

"Never, never! Unless you think me brutal if I ask whether you knew when Linda wrote."

She had an hesitation. "Yes, she showed me her letter. She wouldn't have done anything else. I let it go because I didn't know what course was best. I'm afraid to oppose her to her face."

"Afraid, my dear friend, with that girl?"

"That girl? Much you know about her! It didn't follow you'd come. I didn't take that for granted."

"I'm like you," I said—"I too am afraid of my nephew. I don't venture to oppose him to his face. The only thing I could do—once he wished it—was to come with him."

"I see. Well, there are grounds, after all, on which I'm glad," she rather inscrutably added.

"Oh I was conscientious about that! But I've no authority; I can neither drive him nor stay him—I can use no force," I explained. "Look at the way he's pulling that boat and see if you can fancy me."

"You could tell him she's a bad hard girl—one who'd poison any good man's life!" my companion broke out with a passion that startled me.

At first I could only gape. "Dear lady, what do you mean?"

She bent her face into her hands, covering it over with them, and so remained a minute; then she continued a little differently, though as if she hadn't heard my question: "I hoped you were too disgusted with us—after the way we left you planted."

"It was disconcerting assuredly, and it might have served if Linda hadn't written. That patched it up," I gaily professed. But my gaiety was thin, for I was still amazed at her violence of a moment before. "Do you really mean that she won't do?" I added.

She made no direct answer; she only said after a little that it didn't matter whether the crisis should come a few weeks sooner or a few weeks later, since it was destined to come at the first chance, the favouring moment. Linda had marked my young man—and when Linda had marked a thing!

"Bless my soul—how very grim—" But I didn't understand. "Do you mean she's in love with him?"

"It's enough if she makes him think so—though even that isn't essential."

Still I was at sea. "If she makes him think so? Dear old friend, what's your idea? I've observed her, I've watched her, and when all's said what has she done? She has been civil and pleasant to him, but it would have been much more marked if she hadn't. She has really shown him, with her youth and her natural charm, nothing more than common friendliness. Her note was nothing; he let me see it."

"I don't think you've heard every word she has said to him," Mrs. Pallant returned with an emphasis that still struck me as perverse.

"No more have you, I take it!" I promptly cried. She evidently meant more than she said; but if this excited my curiosity it also moved, in a different connexion, my indulgence.

"No, but I know my own daughter. She's a most remarkable young woman."

"You've an extraordinary tone about her," I declared "such a tone as I think I've never before heard on a mother's lips. I've had the same impression from you—that of a disposition to 'give her away,' but never yet so strong."

At this Mrs. Pallant got up; she stood there looking down at me. "You make my reparation—my expiation—difficult!" And leaving me still more astonished she moved along the terrace.

I overtook her presently and repeated her words. "Your reparation—your expiation? What on earth are you talking about?"

"You know perfectly what I mean—it's too magnanimous of you to pretend you don't."

"Well, at any rate," I said, "I don't see what good it does me, or what it makes up to me for, that you should abuse your daughter."

"Oh I don't care; I shall save him!" she cried as we went, and with an extravagance, as I felt, of sincerity. At the same moment two ladies, apparently English, came toward us—scattered groups had been sitting there and the inmates of the hotel were moving to and fro—and I observed the immediate charming transition, the fruit of such years of social practice, by which, as they greeted us, her tension and her impatience dropped to recognition and pleasure. They stopped to speak to her and she enquired with sweet propriety as to the "continued improvement" of their sister. I strolled on and she presently rejoined me; after which she had a peremptory note. "Come away from this—come down into the garden." We descended to that blander scene, strolled through it and paused on the border of the lake.

V

The charm of the evening had deepened, the stillness was like a solemn expression on a beautiful face and the whole air of the place divine. In the fading light my nephew's boat was too far out to be perceived. I looked for it a little and then, as I gave it up, remarked that from such an excursion as that, on such a lake and at such an hour, a young man and a young woman of common sensibility could only come back doubly pledged to each other.

To this observation Mrs. Pallant's answer was, superficially at least, irrelevant; she said after a pause: "With you, my dear man, one has certainly to dot one's 'i's.' Haven't you discovered, and didn't I tell you at Homburg, that we're miserably poor?"

"Isn't 'miserably' rather too much—living as you are at an expensive hotel?"

Well, she promptly met this. "They take us en pension, for ever so little a day. I've been knocking about Europe long enough to learn all sorts of horrid arts. Besides, don't speak of hotels; we've spent half our life in them and Linda told me only last night that she hoped never to put her foot into one again. She feels that when she comes to such a place as this she ought, if things were decently right, to find a villa of her own."

"Then her companion there's perfectly competent to give her one. Don't think I've the least desire to push them into each other's arms—I only ask to wash my hands of them. But I should like to know why you want, as you said just now, to save him. When you speak as if your daughter were a monster I take it you're not serious."

She was facing me in the rich short twilight, and to describe herself as immeasurably more serious perhaps than she had ever been in her life she had only to look at me without protestation. "It's Linda's standard. God knows I myself could get on! She's ambitious, luxurious, determined to have what she wants—more 'on the make' than any one I've ever seen. Of course it's open to you to tell me it's my own fault, that I was so before her and have made her so. But does that make me like it any better?"

"Dear Mrs. Pallant, you're wonderful, you're terrible," I could only stammer, lost in the desert of my thoughts.

"Oh yes, you've made up your mind about me; you see me in a certain way and don't like the trouble of changing. Votre siège est fait. But you'll HAVE to change—if you've any generosity!" Her eyes shone in the summer dusk and the beauty of her youth came back to her.

"Is this a part of the reparation, of the expiation?" I demanded. "I don't see what you ever did to Archie."

"It's enough that he belongs to you. But it isn't for you I do it—it's for myself," she strangely went on.

"Doubtless you've your own reasons—which I can't penetrate. But can't you sacrifice something else? Must you sacrifice your only child?"

"My only child's my punishment, my only child's my stigma!" she cried in her exaltation.

"It seems to me rather that you're hers."

"Hers? What does SHE know of such things?—what can she ever feel? She's cased in steel; she has a heart of marble. It's true—it's true," said Louisa Pallant. "She appals me!"

I laid my hand on my poor friend's; I uttered, with the intention of checking and soothing her, the first incoherent words that came into my head and I drew her toward a bench a few steps away. She dropped upon it; I placed myself near her and besought her to consider well what she said. She owed me nothing and I wished no one injured, no one denounced or exposed for my sake.

"For your sake? Oh I'm not thinking of you!" she answered; and indeed the next moment I thought my words rather fatuous. "It's a satisfaction to my own conscience—for I HAVE one, little as you may think I've a right to speak of it. I've been punished by my sin itself. I've been hideously worldly, I've thought only of that, and I've taught her to be so—to do the same. That's the only instruction I've ever given her, and she has learned the lesson so well that now I see it stamped there in all her nature, on all her spirit and on all her form, I'm horrified at my work. For years we've lived that way; we've thought of nothing else. She has profited so well by my beautiful influence that she has gone far beyond the great original. I say I'm horrified," Mrs. Pallant dreadfully wound up, "because she's horrible."

"My poor extravagant friend," I pleaded, "isn't it still more so to hear a mother say such things?"

"Why so, if they're abominably true? Besides, I don't care what I say if I save him."

I could only gape again at this least expected of all my adventures. "Do you expect me then to repeat to him—?"

"Not in the least," she broke in; "I'll do it myself." At this I uttered some strong inarticulate protest, but she went on with the grimmest simplicity: "I was very glad at first, but it would have been better if we hadn't met."

"I don't agree to that, for you interest me," I rather ruefully professed, "immensely."

"I don't care if I do—so I interest HIM."

"You must reflect then that your denunciation can only strike me as, for all its violence, vague and unconvincing. Never had a girl less the appearance of bearing such charges out. You know how I've admired her."

"You know nothing about her! *I* do, you see, for she's the work of my hand!" And Mrs. Pallant laughed for bitterness. "I've watched her for years, and little by little, for the last two or three, it has come over me. There's not a tender spot in her whole composition. To arrive at a brilliant social position, if it were necessary, she would see me drown in this lake without lifting a finger, she would stand there and see it—she would push me in—and never feel a pang. That's my young lady!" Her lucidity chilled me to the soul—it seemed to shine so flawless. "To climb up to the top and be splendid and envied there," she went on—"to do that at any cost or by any meanness and cruelty is the only thing she has a heart for. She'd lie for it, she'd steal for it, she'd kill for it!" My companion brought out these words with a cold confidence that had evidently behind it some occult past process of growth. I watched her pale face and glowing eyes; she held me breathless and frowning, but her strange vindictive, or at least retributive, passion irresistibly imposed itself. I found myself at last believing her, pitying her more than I pitied the subject of her dreadful analysis. It was as if she had held her tongue for longer than she could bear, suffering more and more the importunity of the truth. It relieved her thus to drag that to the light, and still she kept up the high and most unholy sacrifice. "God in his mercy has let me see it in time, but his ways are strange that he has let me see it in my daughter. It's myself he has let me see—myself as I was for years. But she's worse—she IS, I assure you; she's worse than I intended or dreamed." Her hands were clasped tightly together in her lap; her low voice quavered and her breath came short; she looked up at the southern stars as if THEY would understand.

"Have you ever spoken to her as you speak to me?" I finally asked. "Have you ever put before her this terrible arraignment?"

"Put it before her? How can I put it before her when all she would have to say would be: 'You, YOU, you base one, who made me—?'"

"Then why do you want to play her a trick?"

"I'm not bound to tell you, and you wouldn't see my point if I did. I should play that boy a far worse one if I were to stay my hand."

Oh I had my view of this. "If he loves her he won't believe a word you say."

"Very possibly, but I shall have done my duty."

"And shall you say to him," I asked, "simply what you've said to me?"

"Never mind what I shall say to him. It will be something that will perhaps helpfully affect him. Only," she added with her proud decision, "I must lose no time."

"If you're so bent on gaining time," I said, "why did you let her go out in the boat with him?"

"Let her? how could I prevent it?"

"But she asked your permission."

"Ah that," she cried, "is all a part of all the comedy!"

It fairly hushed me to silence, and for a moment more she said nothing. "Then she doesn't know you hate her?" I resumed.

"I don't know what she knows. She has depths and depths, and all of them bad. Besides, I don't hate her in the least; I just pity her for what I've made of her. But I pity still more the man who may find himself married to her."

"There's not much danger of there being any such person," I wailed, "at the rate you go on."

"I beg your pardon—there's a perfect possibility," said my companion. "She'll marry—she'll marry 'well.' She'll marry a title as well as a fortune."

"It's a pity my nephew hasn't a title," I attempted the grimace of suggesting.

She seemed to wonder. "I see you think I want that, and that I'm acting a part. God forgive you! Your suspicion's perfectly natural. How can any one TELL," asked Louisa Pallant—"with people like us?"

Her utterance of these words brought tears to my eyes. I laid my hand on her arm, holding her a while, and we looked at each other through the dusk. "You couldn't do more if he were my son."

"Oh if he had been your son he'd have kept out of it! I like him for himself. He's simple and sane and honest—he needs affection."

"He would have quite the most remarkable of mothers-in-law!" I commented.

Mrs. Pallant gave a small dry laugh—she wasn't joking. We lingered by the lake while I thought over what she had said to me and while she herself apparently thought. I confess that even close at her side and under the strong impression of her sincerity, her indifference to the conventional graces, my imagination, my constitutional scepticism began to range. Queer ideas came into my head. Was the comedy on HER side and not on the girl's, and was she posturing as a magnanimous woman at poor Linda's expense? Was she determined, in spite of the young lady's preference, to keep her daughter for a grander personage than a young American whose dollars were not numerous enough—numerous as they were—to make up for his want of high relationships, and had she invented at once the boldest and the subtlest of games in order to keep the case in her hands? If she was prepared really to address herself to Archie she would have to go very far to overcome the mistrust he would be sure to feel at a proceeding superficially so sinister? Was she prepared to go far enough? The answer to these doubts was simply the way I had been touched—it came back to me the next moment—when she used the words "people like us." Their effect was to wring my heart. She seemed to kneel in the dust, and I felt in a manner ashamed that I had let her sink to it. She said to me at last that I must wait no longer, I must go away before the young people came back. They were staying long, too long; all the more reason then she should deal with my nephew that night. I must drive back to Stresa, or if I liked I could go on foot: it wasn't far—for an active man. She disposed of me freely, she was so full of her purpose; and after we had quitted the garden and returned to the terrace above she seemed almost to push me to leave her—I felt her fine consecrated hands fairly quiver on my shoulders. I was ready to do as she prescribed; she affected me painfully, she had given me a "turn," and I wanted to get away from her. But before I went I asked her why Linda should regard my young man as such a parti; it didn't square after all with her account of the girl's fierce ambitions. By that account these favours to one so graceless were a woeful waste of time.

"Oh she has worked it all out; she has regarded the question in every light," said Mrs. Pallant. "If she has made up her mind it's because she sees what she can do."

"Do you mean that she has talked it over with you?"

My friend's wonderful face pitied my simplicity. "Lord! for what do you take us? We don't talk things over to-day. We know each other's point of view and only have to act. We observe the highest proprieties of speech. We never for a moment name anything ugly—we only just go at it. We can take definitions, which are awkward things, for granted."

"But in this case," I nevertheless urged, "the poor thing can't possibly be aware of your point of view."

"No," she conceded—"that's because I haven't played fair. Of course she couldn't expect I'd cheat. There ought to be honour among thieves. But it was open to her to do the same."

"What do you mean by the same?"

"She might have fallen in love with a poor man. Then I should have been 'done.'"

"A rich one's better; he can do more," I replied with conviction.

At this she appeared to have, in the oddest way, a momentary revulsion. "So you'd have reason to know if you had led the life that we have! Never to have had really enough—I mean to do just the few simple things we've wanted; never to have had the sinews of war, I suppose you'd call them, the funds for a campaign; to have felt every day and every hour the hard eternal pinch and found the question of dollars and cents—and so horridly few of them—mixed up with every experience, with every impulse: that DOES make one mercenary, does make money seem a good beyond all others; which it's quite natural it should! And it's why Linda's of the opinion that a fortune's always a fortune. She knows all about that of your nephew, how it's invested, how it may be expected to increase, exactly on what sort of footing it would enable her to live. She has decided that it's enough, and enough is as good as a feast. She thinks she could lead him by the nose, and I dare say she could. She'll of course make him live in these countries; she hasn't the slightest intention of casting her pearls—but basta!" said my friend. "I think she has views upon London, because in England he can hunt and shoot, and that will make him leave her more or less to herself."

"I don't know about his leaving her to herself, but it strikes me that he would like the rest of that matter very much," I returned. "That's not at all a bad programme even from Archie's point of view."

"It's no use thinking of princes," she pursued as if she hadn't heard me. "They're most of them more in want of money even than we. Therefore 'greatness' is out of the question—we really recognised that at an early stage. Your nephew's exactly the sort of young man we've always built upon—if he wasn't, so impossibly, your nephew. From head to foot he was made on purpose. Dear Linda was her mother's own daughter when she recognised him on the spot! One's enough of a prince to-day when one's the right American: such a wonderful price is set on one's not being the wrong! It does as well as anything and it's a great simplification. If you don't believe me go to London and see." She had come with me out to the road. I had said I would walk back to Stresa and we stood there in the sweet dark warmth. As I took her hand, bidding her good-night, I couldn't but exhale a compassion. "Poor Linda, poor Linda!"

"Oh she'll live to do better," said Mrs. Pallant.

"How can she do better—since you've described all she finds Archie as perfection?"

She knew quite what she meant. "Ah better for HIM!"

I still had her hand—I still sought her eyes. "How came it you could throw me over—such a woman as you?"

"Well, my friend, if I hadn't thrown you over how could I do this for you?" On which, disengaging herself, she turned quickly away.

I don't know how deeply she flushed as she made, in the form of her question, this avowal, which was a retraction of a former denial and the real truth, as I permitted myself to believe; but was aware of the colour of my own cheeks while I took my way to Stresa—a walk of half an hour—in the attenuating night. The new and singular character in which she had appeared to me produced in me an emotion that would have made sitting still in a carriage impossible. This same stress kept me up after I had reached my hotel; as I knew I shouldn't sleep it was useless to go to bed. Long, however, as I deferred this ceremony, Archie had not reappeared when the inn-lights began here and there to be dispensed with. I felt even slightly anxious for him, wondering at possible mischances. Then I reflected that in case of an accident on the lake, that is of his continued absence from Baveno—Mrs. Pallant would already have dispatched me a messenger. It was foolish moreover to suppose anything could have happened to him after putting off from Baveno by water to rejoin me, for the evening was absolutely windless and more than sufficiently clear and the lake as calm as glass. Besides I had unlimited confidence in his power to take care of himself in a much tighter place. I went to my room at last; his own was at some distance, the people of the hotel not having been able— it was the height of the autumn season—to make us contiguous. Before I went to bed I had occasion to ring for a servant, and I then learned by a chance enquiry that my nephew had returned an hour before and had gone straight to his own quarters. I hadn't supposed he could come in without my seeing him—I was wandering about the saloons and terraces—and it had not occurred to me to knock at his door. I had half a mind to do so now—I was so anxious as to how I should find him; but I checked myself, for evidently he had wanted to dodge me. This didn't diminish my curiosity, and I slept even less than I had expected. His so markedly shirking our encounter—for if he hadn't perceived me downstairs he might have looked for me in my room— was a sign that Mrs. Pallant's interview with him would really have come off. What had she said to him? What strong measures had she taken? That almost morbid resolution I still seemed to hear the ring of pointed to conceivable extremities that I shrank from considering. She had spoken of these things while we parted there as something she would do for me; but I had made the mental comment in walking away from her that she hadn't done it yet. It wouldn't truly be done till Archie had truly backed out. Perhaps it was done by this time; his avoiding me seemed almost a proof. That was what I thought of most of the night. I spent a considerable part of it at my window, looking out to the couchant Alps. HAD he thought better of it?—was he making up his mind to think better of it? There was a strange contradiction in the matter; there were in fact more contradictions than ever. I had taken from Louisa what she told me of Linda, and yet that other idea made me ashamed of my nephew. I was sorry for the girl; I regretted her loss of a great chance, if loss it was to be; and yet I hoped her mother's grand treachery—I didn't know what to call it—had been at least, to her lover, thoroughgoing. It would need strong action in that lady to justify his retreat. For him too I was sorry—if she had made on him the impression she desired. Once or twice I was on the point of getting into my dressing-gown and going forth to condole with him. I was sure he too had jumped up from his bed and was looking out of his window at the everlasting hills.

But I am bound to say that when we met in the morning for breakfast he showed few traces of ravage. Youth is strange; it has resources that later experience seems only to undermine. One of these is the masterly resource of beautiful blankness. As we grow older and cleverer we think that too simple, too crude; we dissimulate more elaborately, but with an effect much less baffling. My young man looked not in the least as if he had lain awake or had something on his mind; and when I asked him what he had done after my premature departure—I explained this by saying I had been tired of waiting for him; fagged with my journey I had wanted to go to bed—he replied: "Oh nothing in particular. I hung about the place; I like it better than this one. We had an awfully jolly time on the water. *I* wasn't in the least fagged." I didn't worry him with questions; it struck me as gross to try to probe his secret. The only indication he gave was on my saying after breakfast that I should go over again to see our friends and my appearing to take for granted he would be glad to come too. Then he let fall that he'd stop at Stresa—he had paid them such a tremendous visit; also that he had arrears of letters. There was a freshness in his scruples about the length of his visits, and I knew something about his correspondence, which consisted entirely of twenty pages every week from his mother. But he soothed my anxiety so little that it was really this yearning that carried me back to Baveno. This time I ordered a conveyance, and as I got into it he stood watching me from the porch of the hotel with his hands in his pockets. Then it was for the first time that I saw in the poor youth's face the expression of a person slightly dazed, slightly foolish even, to whom something disagreeable has happened. Our eyes met as I observed him, and I was on the point of saying "You had really better come with me" when he turned away. He went into the house as to escape my call. I said to myself that he had been indeed warned off, but that it wouldn't take much to bring him back.

The servant to whom I spoke at Baveno described my friends as in a summer-house in the garden, to which he led the way. The place at large had an empty air; most of the inmates of the hotel were dispersed on the lake, on the hills, in picnics, excursions, visits to the Borromean Islands. My guide was so far right as that Linda was in the summer-house, but she was there alone. On finding this the case I stopped short, rather awkwardly—I might have been, from the way I suddenly felt, an unmasked hypocrite, a proved conspirator against her security and honour. But there was no embarrassment in lovely Linda; she looked up with a cry of pleasure from the book she was reading and held out her hand with engaging frankness. I felt again as if I had no right to that favour, which I pretended not to have noticed. This gave no chill, however, to her pretty manner; she moved a roll of tapestry off the bench so that I might sit down; she praised the place as a delightful shady corner. She had never been fresher, fairer, kinder; she made her mother's awful talk about her a hideous dream. She told me her mother was coming to join her; she had remained indoors to write a letter. One couldn't write out there, though it was so nice in other respects: the table refused to stand firm. They too then had pretexts of letters between them—I judged this a token that the situation was tense. It was the only one nevertheless that Linda gave: like Archie she was young enough to carry it off. She had been used to seeing us always together, yet she made no comment on my having come over without him. I waited in vain for her to speak of this—it would only be natural; her omission couldn't but have a sense. At last I remarked that my nephew was very unsociable that morning; I had expected him to join me, but he hadn't seemed to see the attraction.

"I'm very glad. You can tell him that if you like," said Linda Pallant.

I wondered at her. "If I tell him he'll come at once."

"Then don't tell him; I don't want him to come. He stayed too long last night," she went on, "and kept me out on the water till I don't know what o'clock. That sort of thing isn't done here, you know, and every one was shocked when we came back—or rather, you see, when we didn't! I begged him to bring me in, but he wouldn't. When we did return—I almost had to take the oars myself—I felt as if every one had been sitting up to time us, to stare at us. It was awfully awkward."

These words much impressed me; and as I have treated the reader to most of the reflexions—some of them perhaps rather morbid—in which I indulged on the subject of this young lady and her mother, I may as well complete the record and let him know that I now wondered whether Linda—candid and accomplished maiden—entertained the graceful thought of strengthening her hold of Archie by attempting to prove he had "compromised" her. "Ah no doubt that was the reason he had a bad conscience last evening!" I made answer. "When he came back to Stresa he sneaked off to his room; he wouldn't look me in the face."

But my young lady was not to be ruffled. "Mamma was so vexed that she took him apart and gave him a scolding. And to punish ME she sent me straight to bed. She has very old-fashioned ideas—haven't you, mamma?" she added, looking over my head at Mrs. Pallant, who had just come in behind me.

I forget how her mother met Linda's appeal; Louisa stood there with two letters, sealed and addressed, in her hand. She greeted me gaily and then asked her daughter if she were possessed of postage-stamps. Linda consulted a well-worn little pocket-book and confessed herself destitute; whereupon her mother gave her the letters with the request that she would go into the hotel, buy the proper stamps at the office, carefully affix them and put the letters into the box. She was to pay for the stamps, not have them put on the bill—a preference for which Mrs. Pallant gave reasons. I had bought some at Stresa that morning and was on the point of offering them when, apparently having guessed my intention, the elder lady silenced me with a look. Linda announced without reserve that she hadn't money and Louisa then fumbled for a franc. When she had found and bestowed it the girl kissed her before going off with the letters.

"Darling mother, you haven't any too many of them, have you?" she murmured; and she gave me, sidelong, as she left us, the prettiest half-comical, half-pitiful smile.

"She's amazing—she's amazing," said Mrs. Pallant as we looked at each other.

"Does she know what you've done?"

"She knows I've done something and she's making up her mind what it is. She'll satisfy herself in the course of the next twenty-four hours—if your nephew doesn't come back. I think I can promise you he won't."

"And won't she ask you?"

"Never!"

"Shan't you tell her? Can you sit down together in this summer-house, this divine day, with such a dreadful thing as that between you?"

My question found my friend quite ready. "Don't you remember what I told you about our relations—that everything was implied between us and nothing expressed? The ideas we have had in common—our perpetual worldliness, our always looking out for chances—are not the sort of thing that can be uttered conveniently between persons who like to keep up forms, as we both do: so that, always, if we've understood each other it has been enough. We shall understand each other now, as we've always done, and nothing will be changed. There has always been something between us that couldn't be talked about."

"Certainly, she's amazing—she's amazing," I repeated; "but so are you." And then I asked her what she had said to my boy.

She seemed surprised. "Hasn't he told you?"

"No, and he never will."

"I'm glad of that," she answered simply.

"But I'm not sure he won't come back. He didn't this morning, but he had already half a mind to."

"That's your imagination," my companion said with her fine authority. "If you knew what I told him you'd be sure."

"And you won't let me know?"

"Never, dear friend."

"And did he believe you?"

"Time will show—but I think so."

"And how did you make it plausible to him that you should take so unnatural a course?"

For a moment she said nothing, only looking at me. Then at last: "I told him the truth."

"The truth?"

"Take him away—take him away!" she broke out. "That's why I got rid of Linda, to tell you you mustn't stay—you must leave Stresa to-morrow. This time it's you who must do it. I can't fly from you again—it costs too much!" And she smiled strangely.

"Don't be afraid; don't be afraid. We'll break camp again to-morrow—ah me! But I want to go myself," I added. I took her hand in farewell, but spoke again while I held it. "The way you put it, about Linda, was very bad?"

"It was horrible."

I turned away—I felt indeed that I couldn't stay. She kept me from going to the hotel, as I might meet Linda coming back, which I was far from wishing to do, and showed me another way into the road. Then she turned round to meet her daughter and spend the rest of the morning there with her, spend it before the bright blue lake and the snowy crests of the Alps. When I reached Stresa again I found my young man had gone off to Milan—to see the cathedral, the servant said—leaving a message for me to the effect that, as he shouldn't be back for a day or two, though there were numerous trains, he had taken a few clothes. The next day I received telegram-notice that he had determined to go on to Venice and begged I would forward the rest of his luggage. "Please don't come after me," this missive added; "I want to be alone; I shall do no harm." That sounded pathetic to me, in the light of what I knew, and I was glad to leave him to his own devices. He proceeded to Venice and I re-crossed the Alps. For several weeks after this I expected to discover that he had rejoined Mrs. Pallant; but when we met that November in Paris I saw he had nothing to hide from me save indeed the secret of what our extraordinary friend had said to him. This he concealed from me then and has concealed ever since. He returned to America before Christmas—when I felt the crisis over. I've never again seen the wronger of my youth. About a year after our more recent adventure her daughter Linda married, in London, a young Englishman the heir to a large fortune, a fortune acquired by his father in some prosaic but flourishing industry. Mrs. Gimingham's admired photographs—such is Linda's present name—may be obtained from the principal stationers. I am convinced her mother was sincere. My nephew has not even yet changed his state, my sister at last thinks it high time. I put before her as soon as I next saw her the incidents here recorded, and—such is the inconsequence of women—nothing can exceed her reprobation of Louisa Pallant.

About Author

Henry James OM (15 April 1843 – 28 February 1916) was an American-British author regarded as a key transitional figure between literary realism and literary modernism, and is considered by many to be among the greatest novelists in the English language. He was the son of Henry James Sr. and the brother of renowned philosopher and psychologist William James and diarist Alice James.

He is best known for a number of novels dealing with the social and marital interplay between émigré Americans, English people, and continental Europeans. Examples of such novels include The Portrait of a Lady, The Ambassadors, and The Wings of the Dove. His later works were increasingly experimental. In describing the internal states of mind and social dynamics of his characters, James often made use of a style in which ambiguous or contradictory motives and impressions were overlaid or juxtaposed in the discussion of a character's psyche. For their unique ambiguity, as well as for other aspects of their composition, his late works have been compared to impressionist painting.

His novella The Turn of the Screw has garnered a reputation as the most analysed and ambiguous ghost story in the English language and remains his most widely adapted work in other media. He also wrote a number of other highly regarded ghost stories and is considered one of the greatest masters of the field.

James published articles and books of criticism, travel, biography, autobiography, and plays. Born in the United States, James largely relocated to Europe as a young man and eventually settled in England, becoming a British subject in 1915, one year before his death. James was nominated for the Nobel Prize in Literature in 1911, 1912 and 1916.

Life

Early years, 1843–1883

James was born at 2 Washington Place in New York City on 15 April 1843. His parents were Mary Walsh and Henry James Sr. His father was intelligent and steadfastly congenial. He was a lecturer and philosopher who had inherited independent means from his father, an Albany banker and investor. Mary came from a wealthy family long settled in New York City. Her sister Katherine lived with her adult family for an extended period of time. Henry Jr. had three brothers, William, who was one year his senior, and younger brothers Wilkinson (Wilkie) and Robertson. His younger sister was Alice. Both of his parents were of Irish and Scottish descent.

The family first lived in Albany, at 70 N. Pearl St., and then moved to Fourteenth Street in New York City when James was still a young boy. His education was calculated by his father to expose him to many influences, primarily scientific and philosophical; it was described by Percy Lubbock, the editor of his selected letters, as "extraordinarily haphazard and promiscuous." James did not share the usual education in Latin and Greek classics. Between 1855 and 1860, the James' household traveled to London, Paris, Geneva, Boulogne-sur-Mer and Newport, Rhode Island, according to the father's current interests and publishing ventures, retreating to the United States when funds were low. Henry studied primarily with tutors and briefly attended schools while the family traveled in Europe. Their longest stays were in France, where Henry began to feel at home and became fluent in French. He was afflicted with a stutter, which seems to have manifested itself only when he spoke English; in French, he did not stutter.

In 1860 the family returned to Newport. There Henry became a friend of the painter John La Farge, who introduced him to French literature, and in particular, to Balzac. James later called Balzac his "greatest master," and said that he had learned more about the craft of fiction from him than from anyone else.

In the autumn of 1861 Henry received an injury, probably to his back, while fighting a fire. This injury, which resurfaced at times throughout his life, made him unfit for military service in the American Civil War.

50

In 1864 the James family moved to Boston, Massachusetts to be near William, who had enrolled first in the Lawrence Scientific School at Harvard and then in the medical school. In 1862 Henry attended Harvard Law School, but realised that he was not interested in studying law. He pursued his interest in literature and associated with authors and critics William Dean Howells and Charles Eliot Norton in Boston and Cambridge, formed lifelong friendships with Oliver Wendell Holmes Jr., the future Supreme Court Justice, and with James and Annie Fields, his first professional mentors.

His first published work was a review of a stage performance, "Miss Maggie Mitchell in Fanchon the Cricket," published in 1863. About a year later, A Tragedy of Error, his first short story, was published anonymously. James's first payment was for an appreciation of Sir Walter Scott's novels, written for the North American Review. He wrote fiction and non-fiction pieces for The Nation and Atlantic Monthly, where Fields was editor. In 1871 he published his first novel, Watch and Ward, in serial form in the Atlantic Monthly. The novel was later published in book form in 1878.

During a 14-month trip through Europe in 1869–70 he met Ruskin, Dickens, Matthew Arnold, William Morris, and George Eliot. Rome impressed him profoundly. "Here I am then in the Eternal City," he wrote to his brother William. "At last—for the first time—I live!" He attempted to support himself as a freelance writer in Rome, then secured a position as Paris correspondent for the New York Tribune, through the influence of its editor John Hay. When these efforts failed he returned to New York City. During 1874 and 1875 he published Transatlantic Sketches, A Passionate Pilgrim, and Roderick Hudson. During this early period in his career he was influenced by Nathaniel Hawthorne.

In 1869 he settled in London. There he established relationships with Macmillan and other publishers, who paid for serial installments that they would later publish in book form. The audience for these serialized novels was largely made up of middle-class women, and James struggled to fashion serious literary work within the strictures imposed by editors' and publishers' notions of what was suitable for young women to read. He lived in rented rooms but was able to join gentlemen's clubs that had libraries and where he could entertain male friends. He was introduced to English society by Henry Adams and Charles Milnes Gaskell, the latter introducing him to the Travellers' and the Reform Clubs.

In the fall of 1875 he moved to the Latin Quarter of Paris. Aside from two trips to America, he spent the next three decades—the rest of his life—in Europe. In Paris he met Zola, Alphonse Daudet, Maupassant, Turgenev, and others. He stayed in Paris only a year before moving to London.

In England he met the leading figures of politics and culture. He continued to be a prolific writer, producing The American (1877), The Europeans (1878), a revision of Watch and Ward (1878), French Poets and Novelists (1878), Hawthorne (1879), and several shorter works of fiction. In 1878 Daisy Miller established his fame on both sides of the Atlantic. It drew notice perhaps mostly because it depicted a woman whose behavior is outside the social norms of Europe. He also began his first masterpiece, The Portrait of a Lady, which would appear in 1881.

In 1877 he first visited Wenlock Abbey in Shropshire, home of his friend Charles Milnes Gaskell whom he had met through Henry Adams. He was much inspired by the darkly romantic Abbey and the surrounding countryside, which features in his essay Abbeys and Castles. In particular the gloomy monastic fishponds behind the Abbey are said to have inspired the lake in The Turn of the Screw.

While living in London, James continued to follow the careers of the "French realists", Émile Zola in particular. Their stylistic methods influenced his own work in the years to come. Hawthorne's influence on him faded during this period, replaced by George Eliot and Ivan Turgenev. 1879–1882 saw the publication of The Europeans, Washington Square, Confidence, and The Portrait of a Lady. He visited America in 1882–1883, then returned to London.

The period from 1881 to 1883 was marked by several losses. His mother died in 1881, followed by his father a few months later, and then by his brother Wilkie. Emerson, an old family friend, died in 1882. His friend Turgenev died in 1883.

Middle years, 1884–1897

In 1884 James made another visit to Paris. There he met again with Zola, Daudet, and Goncourt. He had been following the careers of the French "realist" or "naturalist" writers, and was increasingly influenced by them. In 1886, he published The Bostonians and The Princess Casamassima, both influenced by the French writers he'd studied assiduously. Critical reaction and sales were poor. He wrote to Howells that the books had hurt his career rather than helped because they had "reduced the desire, and demand, for my productions to zero". During this time he became friends with Robert Louis Stevenson, John Singer Sargent, Edmund Gosse, George du Maurier, Paul Bourget, and Constance Fenimore Woolson. His third novel from the 1880s was The Tragic Muse. Although he was following the precepts of Zola in his novels of the '80s, their tone and attitude are closer to the fiction of Alphonse Daudet. The lack of critical and financial success for his novels during this period led him to try writing for the theatre. (His dramatic works and his experiences with theatre are discussed below.)

In the last quarter of 1889, he started translating "for pure and copious lucre" Port Tarascon, the third volume of Alphonse Daudet adventures of Tartarin de Tarascon. Serialized in Harper's Monthly Magazine from June 1890, this translation praised as "clever" by The Spectator was published in January 1891 by Sampson Low, Marston, Searle & Rivington.

After the stage failure of Guy Domville in 1895, James was near despair and thoughts of death plagued him. The years spent on dramatic works were not entirely a loss. As he moved into the last phase of his career he found ways to adapt dramatic techniques into the novel form.

In the late 1880s and throughout the 1890s James made several trips through Europe. He spent a long stay in Italy in 1887. In that year the short novel The Aspern Papers and The Reverberator were published.

Late years, 1898–1916

In 1897–1898 he moved to Rye, Sussex, and wrote The Turn of the Screw. 1899–1900 saw the publication of The Awkward Age and The Sacred

Fount. During 1902–1904 he wrote The Ambassadors, The Wings of the Dove, and The Golden Bowl.

In 1904 he revisited America and lectured on Balzac. In 1906–1910 he published The American Scene and edited the "New York Edition", a 24-volume collection of his works. In 1910 his brother William died; Henry had just joined William from an unsuccessful search for relief in Europe on what then turned out to be his (Henry's) last visit to the United States (from summer 1910 to July 1911), and was near him, according to a letter he wrote, when he died.

In 1913 he wrote his autobiographies, A Small Boy and Others, and Notes of a Son and Brother. After the outbreak of the First World War in 1914 he did war work. In 1915 he became a British subject and was awarded the Order of Merit the following year. He died on 28 February 1916, in Chelsea, London. As he requested, his ashes were buried in Cambridge Cemetery in Massachusetts.

Biographers

James regularly rejected suggestions that he should marry, and after settling in London proclaimed himself "a bachelor". F. W. Dupee, in several volumes on the James family, originated the theory that he had been in love with his cousin Mary ("Minnie") Temple, but that a neurotic fear of sex kept him from admitting such affections: "James's invalidism ... was itself the symptom of some fear of or scruple against sexual love on his part." Dupee used an episode from James's memoir A Small Boy and Others, recounting a dream of a Napoleonic image in the Louvre, to exemplify James's romanticism about Europe, a Napoleonic fantasy into which he fled.

Dupee had not had access to the James family papers and worked principally from James's published memoir of his older brother, William, and the limited collection of letters edited by Percy Lubbock, heavily weighted toward James's last years. His account therefore moved directly from James's childhood, when he trailed after his older brother, to elderly invalidism. As more material became available to scholars, including the diaries of contemporaries and hundreds of affectionate and sometimes erotic letters written by James to younger men, the picture of neurotic celibacy gave way to a portrait of a closeted homosexual.

Between 1953 and 1972, Leon Edel authored a major five-volume biography of James, which accessed unpublished letters and documents after Edel gained the permission of James's family. Edel's portrayal of James included the suggestion he was celibate. It was a view first propounded by critic Saul Rosenzweig in 1943. In 1996 Sheldon M. Novick published Henry James: The Young Master, followed by Henry James: The Mature Master (2007). The first book "caused something of an uproar in Jamesian circles" as it challenged the previous received notion of celibacy, a once-familiar paradigm in biographies of homosexuals when direct evidence was non-existent. Novick also criticised Edel for following the discounted Freudian interpretation of homosexuality "as a kind of failure." The difference of opinion erupted in a series of exchanges between Edel and Novick which were published by the online magazine Slate, with the latter arguing that even the suggestion of celibacy went against James's own injunction "live!"—not "fantasize!"

A letter James wrote in old age to Hugh Walpole has been cited as an explicit statement of this. Walpole confessed to him of indulging in "high jinks", and James wrote a reply endorsing it: "We must know, as much as possible, in our beautiful art, yours & mine, what we are talking about — & the only way to know it is to have lived & loved & cursed & floundered & enjoyed & suffered — I don't think I regret a single 'excess' of my responsive youth".

The interpretation of James as living a less austere emotional life has been subsequently explored by other scholars. The often intense politics of Jamesian scholarship has also been the subject of studies. Author Colm Tóibín has said that Eve Kosofsky Sedgwick's Epistemology of the Closet made a landmark difference to Jamesian scholarship by arguing that he be read as a homosexual writer whose desire to keep his sexuality a secret shaped his layered style and dramatic artistry. According to Tóibín such a reading "removed James from the realm of dead white males who wrote about posh people. He became our contemporary."

James's letters to expatriate American sculptor Hendrik Christian Andersen have attracted particular attention. James met the 27-year-old Andersen in Rome in 1899, when James was 56, and wrote letters to Andersen that are intensely emotional: "I hold you, dearest boy, in my innermost love, & count on your feeling me—in every throb of your soul". In a letter of 6 May 1904, to his brother William, James referred to himself as "always your hopelessly celibate even though sexagenarian Henry". How accurate that description might have been is the subject of contention among James's biographers,   but the letters to Andersen were occasionally quasi-erotic: "I put, my dear boy, my arm around you, & feel the pulsation, thereby, as it were, of our excellent future & your admirable endowment." To his homosexual friend Howard Sturgis, James could write: "I repeat, almost to indiscretion, that I could live with you. Meanwhile I can only try to live without you."

His numerous letters to the many young gay men among his close male friends are more forthcoming. In a letter to Howard Sturgis, following a long visit, James refers jocularly to their "happy little congress of two" and in letters to Hugh Walpole he pursues convoluted jokes and puns about their relationship, referring to himself as an elephant who "paws you oh so benevolently" and winds about Walpole his "well meaning old trunk". His letters to Walter Berry printed by the Black Sun Press have long been celebrated for their lightly veiled eroticism.

He corresponded in almost equally extravagant language with his many female friends, writing, for example, to fellow novelist Lucy Clifford: "Dearest Lucy! What shall I say? when I love you so very, very much, and see you nine times for once that I see Others! Therefore I think that—if you want it made clear to the meanest intelligence—I love you more than I love Others." To his New York friend Mary Cadwalader Jones: "Dearest Mary Cadwalader. I yearn over you, but I yearn in vain; & your long silence really breaks my heart, mystifies, depresses, almost alarms me, to the point even of making me wonder if poor unconscious & doting old Célimare [Jones's pet name for James] has 'done' anything, in some dark somnambulism of the spirit, which has ... given you a bad moment, or a wrong impression, or a 'colourable pretext' ... However these things may be, he loves you as tenderly as ever;

nothing, to the end of time, will ever detach him from you, & he remembers those Eleventh St. matutinal intimes hours, those telephonic matinées, as the most romantic of his life ..." His long friendship with American novelist Constance Fenimore Woolson, in whose house he lived for a number of weeks in Italy in 1887, and his shock and grief over her suicide in 1894, are discussed in detail in Edel's biography and play a central role in a study by Lyndall Gordon. (Edel conjectured that Woolson was in love with James and killed herself in part because of his coldness, but Woolson's biographers have objected to Edel's account.)

Works

Style and themes

James is one of the major figures of trans-Atlantic literature. His works frequently juxtapose characters from the Old World (Europe), embodying a feudal civilisation that is beautiful, often corrupt, and alluring, and from the New World (United States), where people are often brash, open, and assertive and embody the virtues—freedom and a more highly evolved moral character—of the new American society. James explores this clash of personalities and cultures, in stories of personal relationships in which power is exercised well or badly. His protagonists were often young American women facing oppression or abuse, and as his secretary Theodora Bosanquet remarked in her monograph Henry James at Work:

> When he walked out of the refuge of his study and into the world and looked around him, he saw a place of torment, where creatures of prey perpetually thrust their claws into the quivering flesh of doomed, defenseless children of light ... His novels are a repeated exposure of this wickedness, a reiterated and passionate plea for the fullest freedom of development, unimperiled by reckless and barbarous stupidity.

Critics have jokingly described three phases in the development of James's prose: "James I, James II, and The Old Pretender." He wrote short stories and plays. Finally, in his third and last period he returned to the long, serialised novel. Beginning in the second period, but most noticeably in the third, he increasingly abandoned direct statement in favour of frequent double negatives, and complex descriptive imagery. Single paragraphs began to run for page after page, in which an initial noun would be succeeded by pronouns surrounded by clouds of adjectives and prepositional clauses, far from their original referents, and verbs would be deferred and then preceded by a series of adverbs. The overall effect could be a vivid evocation of a scene as perceived by a sensitive observer. It has been debated whether this change of style was engendered by James's shifting from writing to dictating to a typist, a change made during the composition of What Maisie Knew.

In its intense focus on the consciousness of his major characters, James's later work foreshadows extensive developments in 20th century fiction. Indeed, he might have influenced stream-of-consciousness writers such as Virginia Woolf, who not only read some of his novels but also wrote essays about them. Both contemporary and modern readers have found the late style difficult and unnecessary; his friend Edith Wharton, who admired him greatly, said that there were passages in his work that were all but incomprehensible. James was harshly portrayed by H. G. Wells as a hippopotamus laboriously attempting to pick up a pea that had got into a corner of its cage. The "late James" style was ably parodied by Max Beerbohm in "The Mote in the Middle Distance".

More important for his work overall may have been his position as an expatriate, and in other ways an outsider, living in Europe. While he came from middle-class and provincial beginnings (seen from the perspective of European polite society) he worked very hard to gain access to all levels of society, and the settings of his fiction range from working class to aristocratic, and often describe the efforts of middle-class Americans to make their way in European capitals. He confessed he got some of his best story ideas from gossip at the dinner table or at country house weekends. He worked for a living, however, and lacked the experiences of select schools, university, and army service, the common bonds of masculine society. He was furthermore a man whose tastes and interests were, according to the prevailing standards of Victorian era Anglo-American culture, rather feminine, and who was shadowed by the cloud of prejudice that then and later accompanied suspicions of his homosexuality. Edmund Wilson famously compared James's objectivity to Shakespeare's:

One would be in a position to appreciate James better if one compared him with the dramatists of the seventeenth century—Racine and Molière, whom he resembles in form as well as in point of view, and even Shakespeare, when allowances are made for the most extreme differences in subject and form. These poets are not, like Dickens and Hardy, writers of melodrama—either humorous or pessimistic, nor secretaries of society like Balzac, nor prophets like Tolstoy: they are occupied simply with the presentation of conflicts of moral character, which they do not concern themselves about softening or averting. They do not indict society for these situations: they regard them as universal and inevitable. They do not even blame God for allowing them: they accept them as the conditions of life.

It is also possible to see many of James's stories as psychological thought-experiments. In his preface to the New York edition of The American he describes the development of the story in his mind as exactly such: the "situation" of an American, "some robust but insidiously beguiled and betrayed, some cruelly wronged, compatriot..." with the focus of the story being on the response of this wronged man. The Portrait of a Lady may be an experiment to see what happens when an idealistic young woman suddenly becomes very rich. In many of his tales, characters seem to exemplify alternative futures and possibilities, as most markedly in "The Jolly Corner", in which the protagonist and a ghost-doppelganger live alternative American and European lives; and in others, like The Ambassadors, an older James seems fondly to regard his own younger self facing a crucial moment.

Major novels

The first period of James's fiction, usually considered to have culminated in The Portrait of a Lady, concentrated on the contrast between Europe and America. The style of these novels is generally straightforward and, though personally characteristic, well within the norms of 19th-century fiction. Roderick Hudson (1875) is a Künstlerroman that traces the development of the title character, an extremely talented sculptor. Although the book shows some signs of immaturity—this was James's first serious attempt at a full-length novel—it has attracted favourable comment due to the vivid realisation of the three major characters: Roderick Hudson, superbly gifted but unstable and unreliable; Rowland Mallet, Roderick's limited but much more mature friend and patron; and Christina Light, one of James's most enchanting and maddening femmes fatales. The pair of Hudson and Mallet has been seen as representing the two sides of James's own nature: the wildly imaginative artist and the brooding conscientious mentor.

In The Portrait of a Lady (1881) James concluded the first phase of his career with a novel that remains his most popular piece of long fiction. The story is of a spirited young American woman, Isabel Archer, who "affronts her destiny" and finds it overwhelming. She inherits a large amount of money and subsequently becomes the victim of Machiavellian scheming by two American expatriates. The narrative is set mainly in Europe, especially in England and Italy. Generally regarded as the masterpiece of his early phase, The Portrait of a Lady is described as a psychological novel, exploring the minds of his characters, and almost a work of social science, exploring the differences between Europeans and Americans, the old and the new worlds.

The second period of James's career, which extends from the publication of The Portrait of a Lady through the end of the nineteenth century, features less popular novels including The Princess Casamassima, published serially in The Atlantic Monthly in 1885–1886, and The Bostonians, published serially in The Century Magazine during the same period. This period also featured James's celebrated Gothic novella, The Turn of the Screw.

The third period of James's career reached its most significant achievement in three novels published just around the start of the 20th century: The Wings of the Dove (1902), The Ambassadors (1903), and The Golden Bowl (1904). Critic F. O. Matthiessen called this "trilogy" James's major phase, and these novels have certainly received intense critical study. It was the second-written of the books, The Wings of the Dove (1902) that was the first published because it attracted no serialization. This novel tells the story of Milly Theale, an American heiress stricken with a serious disease, and her impact on the people around her. Some of these people befriend Milly with honourable motives, while others are more self-interested. James stated in his autobiographical books that Milly was based on Minny Temple, his beloved cousin who died at an early age of tuberculosis. He said that he attempted in the novel to wrap her memory in the "beauty and dignity of art".

Shorter narratives

James was particularly interested in what he called the "beautiful and blest nouvelle", or the longer form of short narrative. Still, he produced a number of very short stories in which he achieved notable compression of sometimes complex subjects. The following narratives are representative of James's achievement in the shorter forms of fiction.

- "A Tragedy of Error" (1864), short story

- "The Story of a Year" (1865), short story

- A Passionate Pilgrim (1871), novella

- Madame de Mauves (1874), novella

- Daisy Miller (1878), novella

- The Aspern Papers (1888), novella

- The Lesson of the Master (1888), novella

- The Pupil (1891), short story

- "The Figure in the Carpet" (1896), short story

- The Beast in the Jungle (1903), novella

- An International Episode (1878)

- Picture and Text

- Four Meetings (1885)

- A London Life, and Other Tales (1889)

- The Spoils of Poynton (1896)

- Embarrassments (1896)

- The Two Magics: The Turn of the Screw, Covering End (1898)

- A Little Tour of France (1900)

- The Sacred Fount (1901)

- Views and Reviews (1908)

- The Wings of the Dove, Volume I (1902)

- The Wings of the Dove, Volume II (1909)

- The Finer Grain (1910)

- The Outcry (1911)

- Lady Barbarina: The Siege of London, An International Episode and Other Tales (1922)

- The Birthplace (1922)

Plays

At several points in his career James wrote plays, beginning with one-act plays written for periodicals in 1869 and 1871 and a dramatisation of his popular novella Daisy Miller in 1882. From 1890 to 1892, having received a bequest that freed him from magazine publication, he made a strenuous effort to succeed on the London stage, writing a half-dozen plays of which only one, a dramatisation of his novel The American, was produced. This play was performed for several years by a touring repertory company and had a respectable run in London, but did not earn very much money for James. His other plays written at this time were not produced.

In 1893, however, he responded to a request from actor-manager George Alexander for a serious play for the opening of his renovated St. James's Theatre, and wrote a long drama, Guy Domville, which Alexander produced. There was a noisy uproar on the opening night, 5 January 1895, with hissing from the gallery when James took his bow after the final curtain, and the author was upset. The play received moderately good reviews and had a modest run of four weeks before being taken off to make way for Oscar Wilde's The Importance of Being Earnest, which Alexander thought would have better prospects for the coming season.

After the stresses and disappointment of these efforts James insisted that he would write no more for the theatre, but within weeks had agreed to write a curtain-raiser for Ellen Terry. This became the one-act "Summersoft", which he later rewrote into a short story, "Covering End", and then expanded into a full-length play, The High Bid, which had a brief run in London in 1907, when James made another concerted effort to write for the stage. He wrote three new plays, two of which were in production when the death of Edward VII on 6 May 1910 plunged London into mourning and theatres closed. Discouraged by failing health and the stresses of theatrical work, James did not renew his efforts in the theatre, but recycled his plays as successful novels. The Outcry was a best-seller in the United States when it was published in 1911. During the years 1890–1893 when he was most engaged with the theatre, James wrote a good deal of theatrical criticism and assisted Elizabeth Robins and others in translating and producing Henrik Ibsen for the first time in London.

Leon Edel argued in his psychoanalytic biography that James was traumatised by the opening night uproar that greeted Guy Domville, and that it plunged him into a prolonged depression. The successful later novels, in Edel's view, were the result of a kind of self-analysis, expressed in fiction, which partly freed him from his fears. Other biographers and scholars have not accepted this account, however; the more common view being that of F.O. Matthiessen, who wrote: "Instead of being crushed by the collapse of his hopes [for the theatre]... he felt a resurgence of new energy."

Non-fiction

Beyond his fiction, James was one of the more important literary critics in the history of the novel. In his classic essay The Art of Fiction (1884), he argued against rigid prescriptions on the novelist's choice of subject and method of treatment. He maintained that the widest possible freedom in content and approach would help ensure narrative fiction's continued vitality.

James wrote many valuable critical articles on other novelists; typical is his book-length study of Nathaniel Hawthorne, which has been the subject of critical debate. Richard Brodhead has suggested that the study was emblematic of James's struggle with Hawthorne's influence, and constituted an effort to place the elder writer "at a disadvantage." Gordon Fraser, meanwhile, has suggested that the study was part of a more commercial effort by James to introduce himself to British readers as Hawthorne's natural successor.

When James assembled the New York Edition of his fiction in his final years, he wrote a series of prefaces that subjected his own work to searching, occasionally harsh criticism.

At 22 James wrote The Noble School of Fiction for The Nation's first issue in 1865. He would write, in all, over 200 essays and book, art, and theatre reviews for the magazine.

For most of his life James harboured ambitions for success as a playwright. He converted his novel The American into a play that enjoyed modest returns in the early 1890s. In all he wrote about a dozen plays, most of which went unproduced. His costume drama Guy Domville failed disastrously on its opening night in 1895. James then largely abandoned his efforts to conquer the stage and returned to his fiction. In his Notebooks he maintained that his theatrical experiment benefited his novels and tales by helping him dramatise his characters' thoughts and emotions. James produced a small but valuable amount of theatrical criticism, including perceptive appreciations of Henrik Ibsen.

With his wide-ranging artistic interests, James occasionally wrote on the visual arts. Perhaps his most valuable contribution was his favourable assessment of fellow expatriate John Singer Sargent, a painter whose critical status has improved markedly in recent decades. James also wrote sometimes charming, sometimes brooding articles about various places he visited and lived in. His most famous books of travel writing include Italian Hours (an example of the charming approach) and The American Scene (most definitely on the brooding side).

James was one of the great letter-writers of any era. More than ten thousand of his personal letters are extant, and over three thousand have been published in a large number of collections. A complete edition of James's letters began publication in 2006, edited by Pierre Walker and Greg Zacharias. As of 2014, eight volumes have been published, covering the period from 1855 to 1880. James's correspondents included celebrated contemporaries like Robert Louis Stevenson, Edith Wharton and Joseph Conrad, along with many others in his wide circle of friends and acquaintances. The letters range from the "mere twaddle of graciousness" to serious discussions of artistic, social and personal issues.

Very late in life James began a series of autobiographical works: A Small Boy and Others, Notes of a Son and Brother, and the unfinished The Middle Years. These books portray the development of a classic observer who was passionately interested in artistic creation but was somewhat reticent about participating fully in the life around him.

Reception

Criticism, biographies and fictional treatments

James's work has remained steadily popular with the limited audience of educated readers to whom he spoke during his lifetime, and has remained firmly in the canon, but, after his death, some American critics, such as Van Wyck Brooks, expressed hostility towards James for his long expatriation and eventual naturalisation as a British subject. Other critics such as E. M. Forster complained about what they saw as James's squeamishness in the treatment of sex and other possibly controversial material, or dismissed his late style as difficult and obscure, relying heavily on extremely long sentences and excessively latinate language. Similarly Oscar Wilde criticised him for writing "fiction as if it were a painful duty". Vernon Parrington, composing a canon of American literature, condemned James for having cut himself off from America. Jorge Luis Borges wrote about him, "Despite the scruples and delicate complexities of James, his work suffers from a major defect: the absence of life." And Virginia Woolf, writing to Lytton Strachey, asked, "Please tell me what you find in Henry James. ... we have his works here, and

I read, and I can't find anything but faintly tinged rose water, urbane and sleek, but vulgar and pale as Walter Lamb. Is there really any sense in it?" The novelist W. Somerset Maugham wrote, "He did not know the English as an Englishman instinctively knows them and so his English characters never to my mind quite ring true," and argued "The great novelists, even in seclusion, have lived life passionately. Henry James was content to observe it from a window." Maugham nevertheless wrote, "The fact remains that those last novels of his, notwithstanding their unreality, make all other novels, except the very best, unreadable." Colm Tóibín observed that James "never really wrote about the English very well. His English characters don't work for me."

Despite these criticisms, James is now valued for his psychological and moral realism, his masterful creation of character, his low-key but playful humour, and his assured command of the language. In his 1983 book, The Novels of Henry James, Edward Wagenknecht offers an assessment that echoes Theodora Bosanquet's:

> "To be completely great," Henry James wrote in an early review, "a work of art must lift up the heart," and his own novels do this to an outstanding degree ... More than sixty years after his death, the great novelist who sometimes professed to have no opinions stands foursquare in the great Christian humanistic and democratic tradition. The men and women who, at the height of World War II, raided the secondhand shops for his out-of-print books knew what they were about. For no writer ever raised a braver banner to which all who love freedom might adhere.

William Dean Howells saw James as a representative of a new realist school of literary art which broke with the English romantic tradition epitomised by the works of Charles Dickens and William Makepeace Thackeray. Howells wrote that realism found "its chief exemplar in Mr. James... A novelist he is not, after the old fashion, or after any fashion but his own." F.R. Leavis championed Henry James as a novelist of "established pre-eminence" in The Great Tradition (1948), asserting that The Portrait of a Lady and The Bostonians were "the two most brilliant novels in the language." James is now prized as a master of point of view who moved literary fiction forward by insisting in showing, not telling, his stories to the reader. (Source: Wikipedia)

NOTABLE WORKS

NOVELS

Watch and Ward (1871)

Roderick Hudson (1875)

The American (1877)

The Europeans (1878)

Confidence (1879)

Washington Square (1880)

The Portrait of a Lady (1881)

The Bostonians (1886)

The Princess Casamassima (1886)

The Reverberator (1888)

The Tragic Muse (1890)

The Other House (1896)

The Spoils of Poynton (1897)

What Maisie Knew (1897)

The Awkward Age (1899)

The Sacred Fount (1901)

The Wings of the Dove (1902)

The Ambassadors (1903)

The Golden Bowl (1904)

The Whole Family (collaborative novel with eleven other authors, 1908)

The Outcry (1911)

The Ivory Tower (unfinished, published posthumously 1917)

The Sense of the Past (unfinished, published posthumously 1917)

SHORT STORIES AND NOVELLAS

A Tragedy of Error (1864)

The Story of a Year (1865)

A Landscape Painter (1866)

A Day of Days (1866)

My Friend Bingham (1867)

Poor Richard (1867)

The Story of a Masterpiece (1868)

A Most Extraordinary Case (1868)

A Problem (1868)

De Grey: A Romance (1868)

Osborne's Revenge (1868)

The Romance of Certain Old Clothes (1868)

A Light Man (1869)

Gabrielle de Bergerac (1869)

Travelling Companions (1870)

A Passionate Pilgrim (1871)

At Isella (1871)

Master Eustace (1871)

Guest's Confession (1872)

The Madonna of the Future (1873)

The Sweetheart of M. Briseux (1873)

The Last of the Valerii (1874)

Madame de Mauves (1874)

Adina (1874)

Professor Fargo (1874)

Eugene Pickering (1874)

Benvolio (1875)

Crawford's Consistency (1876)

The Ghostly Rental (1876)

Four Meetings (1877)

Rose-Agathe (1878, as Théodolinde)

Daisy Miller (1878)

Longstaff's Marriage (1878)

An International Episode (1878)

The Pension Beaurepas (1879)

A Diary of a Man of Fifty (1879)

A Bundle of Letters (1879)

The Point of View (1882)

The Siege of London (1883)

Impressions of a Cousin (1883)

Lady Barberina (1884)

Pandora (1884)

The Author of Beltraffio (1884)

Georgina's Reasons (1884)

A New England Winter (1884)

The Path of Duty (1884)

Mrs. Temperly (1887)

Louisa Pallant (1888)

The Aspern Papers (1888)

The Liar (1888)

The Modern Warning (1888, originally published as The Two Countries)

A London Life (1888)

The Patagonia (1888)

The Lesson of the Master (1888)

The Solution (1888)

The Pupil (1891)

Brooksmith (1891)

The Marriages (1891)

The Chaperon (1891)

Sir Edmund Orme (1891)

Nona Vincent (1892)

The Real Thing (1892)

The Private Life (1892)

Lord Beaupré (1892)

The Visits (1892)

Sir Dominick Ferrand (1892)

Greville Fane (1892)

Collaboration (1892)

Owen Wingrave (1892)

The Wheel of Time (1892)

The Middle Years (1893)

The Death of the Lion (1894)

The Coxon Fund (1894)

The Next Time (1895)

Glasses (1896)

The Altar of the Dead (1895)

The Figure in the Carpet (1896)

The Way It Came (1896, also published as The Friends of the Friends)

The Turn of the Screw (1898)

Covering End (1898)

In the Cage (1898)

John Delavoy (1898)

The Given Case (1898)

Europe (1899)

The Great Condition (1899)

The Real Right Thing (1899)

Paste (1899)

The Great Good Place (1900)

Maud-Evelyn (1900)

Miss Gunton of Poughkeepsie (1900)

The Tree of Knowledge (1900)

The Abasement of the Northmores (1900)

The Third Person (1900)

The Special Type (1900)

The Tone of Time (1900)

Broken Wings (1900)

The Two Faces (1900)

Mrs. Medwin (1901)

The Beldonald Holbein (1901)

The Story in It (1902)

Flickerbridge (1902)

The Birthplace (1903)

The Beast in the Jungle (1903)

The Papers (1903)

Fordham Castle (1904)

Julia Bride (1908)

The Jolly Corner (1908)

The Velvet Glove (1909)

Mora Montravers (1909)

Crapy Cornelia (1909)

The Bench of Desolation (1909)

A Round of Visits (1910)

OTHER

Transatlantic Sketches (1875)

French Poets and Novelists (1878)

Hawthorne (1879)

Portraits of Places (1883)

A Little Tour in France (1884)

Partial Portraits (1888)

Essays in London and Elsewhere (1893)

Picture and Text (1893)

Terminations (1893)

Theatricals (1894)

Theatricals: Second Series (1895)

Guy Domville (1895)

The Soft Side (1900)

William Wetmore Story and His Friends (1903)

The Better Sort (1903)

English Hours (1905)

The Question of our Speech; The Lesson of Balzac. Two Lectures (1905)

The American Scene (1907)

Views and Reviews (1908)

Italian Hours (1909)

A Small Boy and Others (1913)

Notes on Novelists (1914)

Notes of a Son and Brother (1914)

Within the Rim (1918)

Travelling Companions (1919)

Notebooks (various, published posthumously)

The Middle Years (unfinished, published posthumously 1917)

A Most Unholy Trade (1925, published posthumously)

The Art of the Novel : Critical Prefaces (1934)

CPSIA information can be obtained
at www.ICGtesting.com
Printed in the USA
BVHW031426191020
591337BV00001B/483